THE QUEST OF
DANGER

ALSO BY
STUART GIBBS

THE QUEST OF DANGER

ONCE UPON A TIM
BOOK 4

STUART GIBBS

ILLUSTRATED BY STACY CURTIS

SIMON & SCHUSTER BOOKS FOR YOUNG READERS
NEW YORK   LONDON   TORONTO   SYDNEY   NEW DELHI

SIMON & SCHUSTER BOOKS FOR YOUNG READERS

An imprint of Simon & Schuster Children's Publishing Division

1230 Avenue of the Americas, New York, New York 10020

Text © 2023 by Stuart Gibbs

Illustration © 2023 by Stacy Curtis

Case design by Lucy Ruth Cummins © 2023 by Simon & Schuster, Inc.

SIMON & SCHUSTER BOOKS FOR YOUNG READERS

and related marks are trademarks of Simon & Schuster, Inc.

For information about special discounts for bulk purchases, please contact Simon & Schuster Special Sales at 1-866-506-1949 or business@simonandschuster.com.

The Simon & Schuster Speakers Bureau can bring authors to your live event. For more information or to book an event, contact the Simon & Schuster Speakers Bureau at 1-866-248-3049 or visit our website at www.simonspeakers.com.

Interior design by Tom Daly

The text for this book was set in Adobe Caslon Pro.

Manufactured in the United States of America

0923 BVG

First Edition

2 4 6 8 10 9 7 5 3 1

Library of Congress Cataloging-in-Publication Data

Names: Gibbs, Stuart, 1969– author. | Curtis, Stacy, illustrator.

Title: The quest of danger / Stuart Gibbs ; illustrated by Stacy Curtis.

Description: First edition. | New York : Simon & Schuster Books for Young Readers, [2023] | Series: Once upon a tim ; book 4 | Audience: Ages 7 to 10. | Audience: Grades 4–6. | Summary: Tim and his friends flee the hazardous Sea of Terror and head toward the city of Atlantis in pursuit of King Neptuna's stolen trident.

Identifiers: LCCN 2022037722 (print) | LCCN 2022037723 (ebook) | ISBN 9781665917476 | ISBN 9781665917490 (ebook)

Subjects: CYAC: Knights and knighthood—Fiction. | Adventure and adventurers—Fiction. | Atlantis (Legendary place)—Fiction. | Humorous stories. | LCGFT: Humorous fiction. | Novels.

Classification: LCC PZ7.G339236 Qu 2023 (print) | LCC PZ7.G339236 (ebook) | DDC [Fic]—dc23

LC record available at https://lccn.loc.gov/2022037722

LC ebook record available at https://lccn.loc.gov/2022037723

THE QUEST OF
DANGER

CHAPTER ONE

Why I Was in Danger

ONCE UPON A TIME...

My friends and I were tied up in a rowboat, about to plunge over a waterfall at the edge of the earth.

I know this is not the way these stories usually begin.

Believe me, I would have been

much happier if our quest had started some other way. Like this, for instance:

ONCE UPON A TIME . . .

There was a brave young knight-in-training named Tim who woke up safe and sound in his nice, comfy bed to find a hot meal of bacon, oatmeal, and more bacon waiting for him.

Unfortunately, that is not what was happening in my life at this time.

Over the past few days, I had battled a bargleboar, a sea monster, *and* a hydra; been tortured by the horrendous singing of the sirens; nearly got swallowed by a giant whirlpool; been betrayed by my fellow knights; and been captured by the evil Prince Ruprecht and his horde of nasty pirates, who had put us in that rowboat and sent us to our doom.

All in all, it was a crummy week.

And yet, being a knight-in-training was still better than my previous job.

Before this, I had been a peasant, just like my father and his father and his father and everyone else in the history of my family. Being a peasant was dull and boring, which is why I had jumped at the chance to become a knight.

Being a knight had been very exciting. Quite a bit more exciting than I had expected, in fact. I had traveled to many distant lands, met many unusual people, and nearly died in many different ways.

Obviously, I had survived all those ordeals. But this one looked like it might be different.

You may have noticed that there were three other people and a giant frog in the boat with me.

Belinda was my closest friend, a tough, loyal girl who had pretended to be a boy so that she could join the knights, because, sadly, most people in my time didn't think girls could do anything except be housewives or witches.

Princess Grace was, well . . . a princess. The princess of Merryland. People in my time (including Princess Grace's parents) thought that princesses should do even less than other girls. They were expected to simply wait around the castle for princes to show up and ask to marry them. Princess Grace liked the idea of that even less than Belinda and I liked the idea of being peasants, so she had snuck away to join us on our adventure.

Of course, if she had known how things were going to work out, she might have stayed home.

Ferkle was our village idiot, although he was actually very intelligent. He had only gone into village idiocy because it was the family business.

Rover was not really a giant frog. He was a fr-dog. He had originally been my dog, until the mean witch who lived next door to me got angry at him for digging up her begonias and turned him into a frog. So now he was a frog who behaved like a dog. He could lick your face from ten feet away.

I'm not sure if Rover was worried about the waterfall ahead, but the rest of us certainly were. We had almost reached the lip of it and were about to go over the edge of the earth.

"I know we have been in plenty of danger before," Ferkle said, "and we have escaped each time. But this situation doesn't look very good at all."

"So you don't have a plan for how to get us out of this?" Princess Grace asked.

"If I had a plan to get us out of this," Ferkle said, "don't you think I would have put it into action already?"

Princess Grace frowned. "I was hoping that, maybe, you were waiting until the last moment to announce it. For better dramatic effect."

"No," Ferkle told her. "In fact, there's really only one thing I can come up with to do right now."

"What's that?" Belinda asked.

"Cry," Ferkle replied. And then he began to sob. "It's not fair! We're all too young to die!"

Princess Grace and Belinda began to cry as well. I felt that I ought to try to be brave and strong in the moment, but I found myself getting teary too.

The current took the boat to the edge of the waterfall. Our bow poked over the rim. We were only a second away from plunging to our doom.

And then we stopped.

The water kept flowing all around us, but our boat was no longer moving. We just sat there with the stern in the water and the bow sticking out over the edge of a very, very, very big drop.

You are probably not that surprised that we didn't go over. I mean, this is only the first chapter of the book. There's still over a hundred pages left. If we were going to perish right off the bat, then this would only be a pamphlet.

However, my friends and I were *very* surprised.

"What happened?" I asked, feeling extremely relieved but still quite nervous. "Why aren't we plummeting to our deaths?"

"I don't know," Ferkle admitted.

"Perhaps it's some sort of magic?" Belinda suggested.

"Maybe the person whose hand this is could tell us," Princess Grace said.

The rest of us looked at her, confused.

"What hand?" I asked.

"The one holding on to our boat," Princess Grace replied. And then she pointed to it.

Sure enough, there was a hand grasping the stern of the rowboat. Like this:

The hand was attached to a very muscular arm, which was sticking out of the water. The rest of whoever the arm belonged to was hidden below the surface.

And that's when our adventure *really* began.

CHAPTER TWO

Who Had Saved Us

While we were staring at the hand, another emerged from the water beside it. This hand had a large hook in it, although rather than being made out of steel or some other kind of metal, the hook was made out of coral. The hook was at the end of a long rope made out of seaweed.

The second hand fastened the hook to the back of our boat.

Then both hands let go.

For a very scary moment, we moved forward again, nearly toppling over the edge of the waterfall, but then the seaweed rope went taut and we stopped.

At the other end of the rope, two seahorses emerged from the water.

The seahorses swam forward, pulling us away from the edge . . .

Oh wait.

You might be confused about the seahorses.

You're probably thinking about this kind of seahorse:

Very small

Upright Posture

Prehensile tail

Doesn't look a thing like a horse!

This is a weird little tropical fish that swims upright, has a prehensile tail and a really misleading name. Apparently, whoever decided to call them seahorses had never seen an actual horse. While a sea turtle is quite obviously a turtle and a sea otter is certainly an otter, a seahorse doesn't look much like a horse at all. Horses are big, strong, four-legged beasts that can run very fast. The kind of seahorses illustrated before are ridiculously small and frail, have no legs, and are so slow that they often lose races to plankton.

This is the type of seahorse that I'm talking about:

This is clearly a horse that lives in the sea. Half horse. Half fish. I know, it looks a little bit silly—but if you think about it, it's not nearly as silly-looking as what you've been calling a seahorse all this time.

These seahorses were big, strong, and fast enough to easily pull us away from the edge of the waterfall. And then they kept on going, whisking us across the surface of the water. It was as though we were on a chariot designed for the sea.

Once we were a good, safe distance from the waterfall, a woman suddenly leapt out of the water beside us and landed in our boat.

Well . . . really, it was only half a woman. The top half. The bottom half of her was fish.

"Hello!" she said cheerfully. "My name is Piscina!"

We all gaped at her in surprise.

"You're a mermaid!" Princess Grace exclaimed.

Piscina's smile instantly faded. "The term mermaid is sexist," she said, giving Princess Grace a disparaging look. "I prefer the term merperson."

(I'm guessing you noticed that IQ Booster there. On occasion, I'm going to use a word you might not know in this book. But this is really in your best interest, for a couple of reasons: First of all, I will always define the word, so that you will know how to use it afterward. Like this: "disparaging" means "expressing the opinion that something is of little worth." Secondly, sometimes teachers or parents think that hilarious books with pictures in them—like this one—aren't as educational as books without pictures that are about serious subjects like human rights and foot fungus. But with these handy IQ Boosters, you can prove that this book *is* educational. So if a teacher or parent notices you reading this book and suggests that maybe your time would be better spent reading something else, just tell them, "I would appreciate it if you wouldn't be so disparaging of my choice of reading material. This book is really very educational and is helping me expand my vocabulary." Of course, that teacher or parent will immediately apologize and encourage you to continue reading.)

Princess Grace was a kind and good-hearted person, and so she was very embarrassed to have upset Piscina's feelings. "I'm so sorry!" she said. "I didn't mean to offend you! And by the way, thank you for saving our lives."

"You're welcome," Piscina replied. She seemed far less upset now that Princess Grace had apologized. "I couldn't just let all of you die. I wish I could have rescued you sooner, but I didn't have a hook or a rope handy and had to make them. I assume you'd like to be untied as well?"

"Yes," Princess Grace replied. "That would be very nice."

Piscina held up a knife that was made from a sharp piece of coral and quickly sawed through the ropes that bound us.

While she did this, we all introduced ourselves. Then we started to explain how we had ended up in such trouble. . . .

"Oh, I know exactly how you got into that predicament," Piscina said. "I saw the whole thing."

(A predicament is a difficult, unpleasant, or embarrassing situation. Piscina had a very impressive vocabulary for someone who was half-fish, probably because the part that was half-fish was not the part with her brain in it. A merperson whose top half is fish has a very limited vocabulary, an extremely short attention span, and the IQ of a cucumber.)

Piscina then reached into the sea and hauled out a mesh bag made of seaweed that she had been dragging along. Inside the bag were five large glass bubbles, each with a hole at the bottom. "I need you to put these over your heads," she told us.

"Why?" I asked.

"So you won't drown when we visit my city," Piscina replied as though it was obvious.

IQ BOOSTER!

Not so smart

Terrible at swimming

All of us examined our glass bubbles curiously (except Rover, of course). They were beautifully made and crystal clear.

We put them over our heads.

Piscina shouted a command to her seahorses in a language I did not know.

The seahorses promptly dove beneath the surface, dragging us down with them.

This really freaked me out.

I had never been beneath the surface of the sea. In fact, I hadn't even *seen* the sea until a few days earlier. All I knew about going beneath the surface was that it was generally a bad idea. There were sharks down there. And sea monsters. And there was no air to breathe.

However, the glass bubbles had enough air to prevent us from drowning. Once I got over the initial shock of going underwater, I saw that it was far more beautiful down there than I had imagined. There were large schools of colorful fish, forests of seaweed, and—on the bottom of the sea itself—there was an entire merperson city.

All of this was very surprising, although the *most* surprising part was that there were other half-fish creatures down there. I had heard legends about merpeople before, but it had never occurred to me that they would have merdogs and mercats as pets, or flocks of merchickens and herds of mercows. It was all surprisingly like our world, except a whole lot wetter.

The merpeople seemed to find us just as strange and fascinating as we found them. The adults stopped and stared at us as we passed, while the children pointed at our legs and giggled.

"Welcome to the Kingdom of Merland!" Piscina announced.

We headed through the city, passing many homes and shops (most of which seemed to be selling a variety of seaweed), until we reached the biggest building in town, a great sandcastle.

"Why are we going here?" Belinda asked curiously.

"Because this is where I live!" Piscina said. "I am the princess of Merland—and my parents want to meet you."

"Why?" Princess Grace asked. She suddenly looked very worried.

"I'll let them tell you," Princess Piscina replied. "Because it's very, very, very important."

Princess Grace gulped.

I wasn't sure why she was worried, but I was feeling anxious too.

I had a sense that there was plenty more danger in store for us.

And sadly, I was right.

CHAPTER THREE

What the Merpeople Wanted

Some mer–stable hands took the seahorses away, and Princess Piscina led us into the castle.

In addition to providing us with air to breathe, the glass bubbles were also heavy, weighting us down and preventing us from floating away. This allowed us to walk along the floor of the sea, which was help-ful, because none of us knew how to swim very well—except Rover. As a frog, he could swim very well, and he immediately chased after some mercats, barking furiously. Unfortunately for Rover, they were still faster than he was—and he couldn't catch them with his tongue because of the glass bubble over his head. He still tried, though, and ended up looking like this:

As we passed through the halls of the castle, I noticed that Princess Grace was growing more worried and miserable with every step.

"What's wrong?" I whispered to her, not wanting Princess Piscina to overhear us.

"They obviously know I'm a princess," Princess Grace replied. "And now they're going to try to marry me off to their son."

"We don't know that for sure," I pointed out.

"It happens all the time," Princess Grace said morosely.

"That's all anyone thinks I'm good for: marriage. They don't care about my mind or my personality or my life goals. Once they hear I'm a princess, they want me to marry their prince."

"Maybe they don't even have a prince," I said.

"Oh, I'm sure they do," Princess Grace replied. "And I'm sure they think he's wonderful. Every king and queen *always* think their son will be the perfect man for me, even if he is a terrible, awful nimrod like Prince Ruprecht. Worse, my parents will probably agree to it. They can't wait to marry me off. No one ever asks me what *I* want."

"What *do* you want?" I asked.

"I want someone who is smart and brave and funny and honorable and attractive." Princess Grace suddenly grew embarrassed and lowered her voice until it was barely audible. "Kind of like your cousin Bull."*

"But Bull is . . . ," I began, and then caught myself before I finished the sentence. I had been about to say *a girl*, but that would have been a big mistake. If the truth

---

* If you haven't read any of the other books in this series, Bull is the name that Belinda used to convince everyone that she was a boy.

had come out that Belinda had lied about being a boy to become a knight, she could have ended up in a lot of trouble. As punishment, she could have been put in a dungeon—being forced to gargle live bees. (The punishment for posing as a boy to become a knight varied greatly from kingdom to kingdom.) At the very least, she would have been kicked off the Knight Brigade and forced to be a peasant again, which Belinda wanted to do even less than gargle live bees. So I had sworn to protect Belinda's secret. Now my mind scrambled quickly to come up with something else. ". . . not a prince," I finished.

"So?" Princess Grace asked.

"Won't your parents be upset if you don't marry a prince?" I asked.

Princess Grace sighed. "Yes. A prince is all they care about. Even if the prince is half-flounder and I have to live at the bottom of the sea with a glass bubble over my head for the rest of my life."

She hung her head and continued through the castle.

I heaved a sigh of relief so big that it fogged up my

glass bubble, thankful that I hadn't revealed the truth
about Belinda. Although I also felt bad for Princess Grace.
When I had first met her, marrying a prince was her only
goal in life. Obviously that had changed—and part of that
change was due to Belinda encouraging her to stand up
for herself.

I found myself hoping that the prince of Merland
would turn out to be a really good guy. Maybe he would
be smart and brave and funny and honorable and attractive. Maybe the half of him that was fish would be a *cool*
fish, like a shark. And then Princess Grace would fall for
him and forget all about Belinda, and I would never have
to reveal the truth.

But that is not what happened.

We arrived at the throne room to find the king and
queen of Merland seated on large, fancy thrones. They
wore large, fancy crowns. The queen held a large, fancy
golden scepter, while the king held a trident that wasn't
remotely large and fancy at all. Instead, it was kind of
crummy: a few twigs that had been poorly tied together.

There was no prince anywhere to be seen.

"Greetings!" the king thundered. "I am Neptuna, King of Merland. This is my wife, Gilly, Queen of Merland. And you have already met Princess Piscina. Thank you for coming."

I expected that Princess Grace would say something in response, but she was still sulking. Then I looked to Ferkle, hoping he might step up. Only, since we were in front of other people, Ferkle had resumed his duties as village idiot and was putting some crabs down his pants. I then looked to Belinda, who motioned that I should handle this. So I stepped forward and said, "Thank you for having us. I am Sir Tim, this is Sir Bull, this is the fair Princess Grace, and this is our village idiot, Ferkle."

"Hello," said Belinda.

"Blurk," said Ferkle.

Princess Grace didn't say anything at all. She just waved meekly.

"We are well aware of who you are," King Neptuna said. "We have been watching your adventures at sea. You have proven yourselves to be very brave and honorable, unlike the other knights you were sailing with."

"Oh. You saw them abandon us?" I asked. When Prince Ruprecht had given the elder knights of Merryland the choice of joining him or fighting against his superior force to protect Princess Grace, they had quickly surrendered and switched sides.

"Yes," King Neptuna said with obvious disgust. "Those men behaved in a manner that was odious and despicable." ← DOUBLE IQ BOOSTER!

THE QUEST OF DANGER   29

("Odious" and "despicable" mean "really, really, really awful." King Neptuna probably could have simply said one or the other, but saying both at the same time really got the point across.)

"And yet," King Neptuna continued, "the behavior of Prince Ruprecht was even worse. It is because of him that I brought you here."

"What did he do to you?" I asked.

"He has stolen the Great Trident of Merland!" King Neptuna roared. "Which is why I'm holding this cheap imitation instead!" He shook the spindly homemade trident so angrily that one of the three prongs came loose and floated away. "Oh nuts," King Neptuna muttered.

I thought back to the last time we had seen Prince Ruprecht. My friends and I had just defeated the hydra and recovered many treasures that the Kingdom of Dinkum had stolen. And then, while we were exhausted from the battle, Prince Ruprecht had come along and stolen the treasures from us. There had been a lot of treasures, but I recalled briefly seeing the trident, which was big and golden and studded with precious gems.

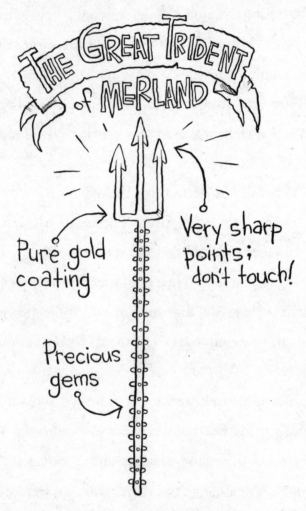

Belinda said, "I know that Ruprecht stole the trident from us, but didn't the Kingdom of Dinkum steal it from you first?"

"Yes!" King Neptuna shouted. "They are even more odious and despicable than Ruprecht! I hate the Dingdum of Kinkum! I mean, the Binkbum of Sinkum! I mean, the Flingflum of Pinkgum! I mean . . . whatever the heck it's called! But since Ruprecht has the trident now, he's the one we want you to go after. I need you to find him and get my trident back."

"Us?" I asked, concerned. "But Ruprecht hates us and has tried to kill us many times. In fact, he would have killed us if Piscina hadn't saved us from going over the waterfall. Which is definitely going to make him even angrier. Plus, Ruprecht now has a great horde of pirates working for him—as well as all the elder knights of Merryland—while there are only five of us—one of which is a fr-dog."

"Perhaps," said Queen Gilly. "But you are all very brave— and we *can't* go after him, because we don't have legs."

"Isn't he on a ship?" Belinda asked.

"He *was*," King Neptuna reported. "But my spies tell me he has taken the trident to the city of Atlantis."

Ferkle, Belinda, Princess Grace, and I all gasped in amazement.

I know that, in your time, Atlantis is famous for being a sunken city, but in *my* time, that had not happened yet. Back then, Atlantis was famous for being the most beautiful, wealthy, and glorious city that anyone had ever seen.

"What is Ruprecht doing in Atlantis?" I asked.

"That's for you to find out," King Neptuna replied. "Feel free to ask him after you have stolen my trident back."

"So then . . . ," Princess Grace said. "This is all just about the trident?"

"Of course it's about the trident!" Neptuna snapped. "What else would I have brought you down here for?"

"Well, I *am* a princess," Princess Grace replied. "And lots of the times, kings and queens want me to marry their sons."

King Neptuna burst out laughing. So did Queen Gilly. "Why would we want our son to marry you?" Neptuna scoffed. "You're not the slightest bit fish! You have those silly limbs coming out of your bottom instead of a tail! They look ridiculous! You can probably barely even swim with them!"

"That's true," Princess Grace admitted. I had thought she would be relieved to hear that there was no prince for her to marry, but now she simply looked embarrassed.

King Neptuna said, "My only interest is in your ability to get my trident back. And the sooner you do that, the better. So get on with it." He waved his hand, as if shooing us from the room.

"But we haven't actually *agreed* to go after the trident," Belinda reminded him.

King Neptuna stopped in mid-shoo, realizing she was right. "Ah yes. I suppose that's true. Well, let's discuss that. If you go retrieve my trident, I will be very pleased and will reward you handsomely for your efforts. But if you don't go retrieve my trident, then I will be very upset and have no choice but to return you to the exact spot where I found you."

Belinda grew worried. "You mean, about to fall over the waterfall at the edge of the world?"

"That's correct," said the king.

"In that case," Belinda said, "we'd be happy to help."

CHAPTER FOUR

Where We Were Going

"Sorry about my father," Princess Piscina said. "He isn't usually that curmudgeonly." ⟨ IQ BOOSTER! |

("Curmudgeonly" means "grumpy or grouchy." As in: "My curmudgeonly schoolteacher didn't like it when I laughed out loud at the hilarious book I was reading.")

Piscina was leading us back through the castle from the throne room. "Dad's really upset about his trident," she explained. "It's not just pretty and expensive. It also has magical powers. With it, you can get any sea creature to do your bidding."

Belinda, Ferkle, and I all shared a look of surprise. A trident that could control all the creatures of the sea would be powerful indeed.

"Ooh!" Princess Grace said. "That sounds lovely!"

"It is," Piscina agreed. "The trident has been the pride of Merland for as long as anyone can remember. All the merpeople were devastated when it was stolen. Many of us tried to get it back from the Kingdom of Dinkum, but they kept it on land, so us not having legs was a problem."

Princess Grace asked, "Couldn't you get a sea witch to do some kind of magic that would give you legs for a while?"

Piscina gave her a look of disgust. "First of all, no. That's not possible. And second of all, ick. No offense, but legs are weird."

Princess Grace *did* take offense, and it looked like she was about to say something like, *They're better than having some stinky, floppy fish tail.* So before an argument broke out, I interrupted.

"How are we even supposed to get to Atlantis?" I asked.

"You can take your rowboat and borrow our seahorses to pull it," Piscina replied.

"But we don't even know how to get there," Belinda added.

"I have a map!" Piscina exclaimed. Then she held it out for us to see.

As maps went, it was pretty bad. Instead of being on paper, it was on a rock. And the words were very poorly written.

"Sorry for the quality," Piscina apologized. "Paper doesn't last very long down here, so we have to use rocks. Which means that a really long book can weigh six tons. And the only ink we have is squid ink."

"I've heard that squid ink is actually very good ink," Belinda noted.

"Oh it is," Piscina agreed. "But squid have terrible handwriting."

We all gathered around to have a better look at the map.

Looking at it, I felt very worried.

I had heard of the kraken. It was a huge sea monster that could swallow ships whole. We had run into a horrifying sea monster named Scylla on our way to Dinkum. Well, even Scylla was said to be afraid of the kraken.

I had also heard of cyclopes. They were angry one-eyed giants who tried to smash anything they saw. Including people.

"This seems really, really dangerous," I said.

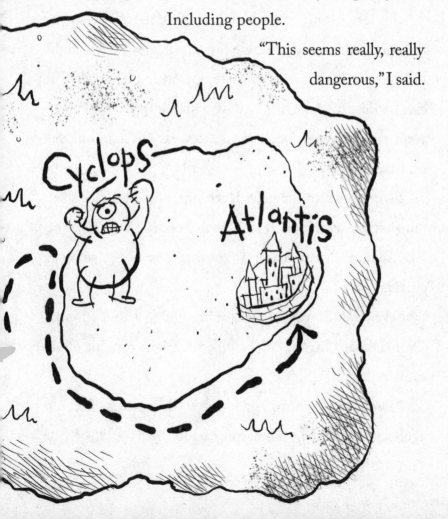

"No kidding," Belinda agreed. "Just thinking about this quest is making my blood go cold."

"Actually, that's happening because you're losing body heat to the water," Ferkle observed. "It's called hypothermia. ◁ IQ BOOSTER! We've all been down at the bottom of the sea for way too long."

(I guess I don't really have to define the word "hypothermia" here, because Ferkle just did it. But he was right to be concerned. If your body temperature gets too low, it can be deadly. Which is why you should always listen to your parents when they tell you to wear a hat and gloves on a cold day.)

I looked at my friends. Everyone now had a slightly bluish tint, which indicated that Ferkle knew what he was talking about. Being at the bottom of the sea was chilling us.

"We should probably get going, then," I told Piscina. "Not only am I cold, but I think we might run out of air soon."

"Then you ought to head back to the surface," Piscina agreed. "It would be very unfortunate to have all of you

asphyxiate ⟨ IQ BOOSTER! ⟩ before you even have the chance
to get our trident back."

(To asphyxiate is to die as a result of not having any
air. I was in complete agreement with her about this being
unfortunate.)

We exited the sandcastle and found the seahorses and
our rowboat waiting for us. Piscina handed me the map,
which was very heavy, even underwater. "Use this to guide
you to Atlantis and then to find your way back here again.
Thank you for bravely volunteering to help us and going
on this dangerous quest."

"Actually, we *didn't* volunteer," I pointed out. "You
forced us into doing it."

"I also saved you from certain death," Piscina reminded
me. "So I guess you owed us a favor."

I didn't really agree with this. As far as I was concerned, a favor was something like helping a friend tend
their crops or lending them a cup of gruel. Going on a
long, dangerous journey to recover a magical relic from
your evil nemesis seemed like a bit more than that. But
there was no point in arguing.

I climbed into the rowboat with my friends and whistled to Rover, who was chasing some mersquirrels up a sea tree. My fr-dog swam back into the boat. Ferkle snapped the reins, and the seahorses leapt into action.

They pulled us upward, racing through great schools of fish. Merland dropped away below us, growing smaller and smaller, and then we burst through the surface once again.

We took the glass bubbles off our heads and gulped great breaths of fresh air. The sun was blazing, and our bodies returned to normal temperature. All this reinvigorated ⟨ IQ BOOSTER! ⟩ us.

(To reinvigorate is to give new energy or strength to. Have you ever had a day when you were feeling extra tired and poky, but then heard some good news or had a candy bar and suddenly felt as good as new? That's reinvigoration. It's a very good argument for having candy bars around the house at all times.)

With the fresh air and the warm sun and my friends around me, my spirits quickly lifted. My worries about our journey faded. I began to feel as though we could actually handle this quest without much trouble. I was happy, excited, and enthusiastic.

And then we ran into the kraken.

How to Defeat a Kraken

Like I said, I had heard of the kraken before. It was the sort of thing that your parents told you tales about to terrify you into behaving.

"The kraken is the most foul-smelling, disgusting, and grotesque beast that ever lived," they would say. "And they only eat boys and girls who don't help with their chores."

When I was little, this worked like a charm. I lived in mortal fear of the kraken and did every single thing my parents asked me to.

However, as I grew older, I started to recognize the logic flaws in this story. How could an animal that lived in the darkest depths of the sea come all the way inland to my home to eat me? How would it know that I hadn't done my chores? And why would that make me tastier than anyone else? Frankly, if a sea monster was going to go through the trouble to haul itself all the way to my village, you'd think it would just eat *everyone*.

Eventually, I figured out that my parents were lying to me and then presumed that the kraken was a myth as well. I stopped believing in it. After all, there were plenty of other vicious monsters that really did exist for me to worry about.

But then I saw it.

Or, more specifically, I saw *part* of it.

The thing about sea monsters is you rarely get to see all of them. When a dragon comes flying out of the sky toward you, or a bargleboar charges you across open ground, you can usually get a very good look at it. (In fact, that very good look is often the last thing that many people see in their lives.) But a sea monster lives . . . well, in the sea. And so most times, when you come across one, you only see a small portion of it.

With the kraken, though, that was plenty.

The first part we saw was a claw, which burst through

the surface of the water beside us. It was big and powerful and covered with spikes and other nasty things—and it looked like it could easily slice any one of us in half.

It also was the worst-smelling thing I had ever encountered. I know that, in a previous book, I said that the stinx smelled terrible, but at the time, I had never encountered the kraken. The kraken reeked so badly that a stinx would have been nauseated.

The seahorses whinnied in terror and tried to swim away, but the claw grabbed the rowboat and held on tight. Despite their strength, the seahorses were no match for it. They pulled as hard as they could, but we stayed right where we were.

"Attack!" yelled Ferkle. Now that no one else was around, he didn't feel obligated to behave like the village idiot anymore. He grabbed his sword and stabbed at the claw.

So did the rest of us. But the shell of the claw was thick and impervious ◁ IQ BOOSTER! ▷ to our swords.

("Impervious" means "unaffected by." Usually, it is used in the physical sense: a nice new coat can be impervious to rain. But it is also fun to use metaphorically: a stubborn person can be impervious to new ideas, or a confident person can be impervious to bullying. I am using it in the physical sense: no matter how hard we stabbed the kraken, we couldn't even break its shell. It was like trying to stab through a brick wall with a toothpick.)

Even though we didn't seem to be affecting the claw at all, we still kept hacking away at it, hoping to make something happen.

Then Belinda shouted, "Tim! Behind you!"

I spun around to find *another* claw reaching for me.
I was surprised—although I shouldn't have been. After
all, have you ever seen a creature with only one claw? No.
They all have at least two.

Or, in the case of a kraken, *many*, many more than two.

Suddenly there were claws lashing out everywhere
around us. There were far more claws than there were of

us. And every one of them was impervious to our swords.

We still did our best to hurt them, but the claws quickly got tired of this, grabbed all our swords, and flung them into the sea.

Now we had no weapons to protect ourselves against the increasingly large number of claws.

More of the kraken began to emerge from the sea. Two enormous eyes on long stalks popped out of the water. So did a gaping mouth full of thousands of razor-sharp teeth.

The claws swarmed around us. We did our best to fight them off, punching and kicking, but it was obvious that it wouldn't be long before the claws plucked each one of us off the boat and tossed us into the mouth, which would certainly chew us up in the most painful way possible.

This was the second time in a single day that we were about to die.

But then, just as the claws were ready to grab all of us, Rover decided he'd had enough. He began barking furiously.

Rover had possessed a very loud bark when he was a regular dog. Now, with the great big throat of a frog, it was even louder.

He didn't go "BARK BARK BARK BARK BARK!"

He went "BARK BARK BARK BARK BARK BARK!!!!"

The claws quickly recoiled back toward the water, as though frightened.

"I think the kraken is afraid of loud noises!" Ferkle exclaimed. "So let's make some more!"

We all did exactly what he had suggested. We started shouting at the kraken at the top of our lungs.

"LEAVE US ALONE!" "GO PICK ON SOME-ONE YOUR OWN SIZE!" "YOU STINK!" "WE TASTE REALLY TERRIBLE!"

We weren't nearly as loud as Rover, but we still made quite a racket. And meanwhile, Rover was barking the whole time. So overall, it was a great deal of noise.

The claws wavered a bit, and then they and the giant eyes and the huge gaping mouth all slipped back into the sea, and the kraken quickly swam away.

It had let go of the rowboat, but the seahorses were too exhausted from fighting it to swim anymore, so we stayed right where we were.

All of us sat there for a moment, staring at the water, surprised that our shouting had worked but very relieved as well.

"Wow," Belinda said. "That kraken certainly swam away in a hurry."

"I guess we really scared it off," said Princess Grace.

CHAPTER FIVE AND A HALF

What Had Really Scared the Kraken Off

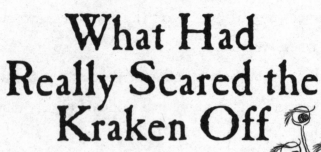

It wasn't us.

CHAPTER SIX

Why You Shouldn't Let Squid Make Maps

It is a little known fact that squid make lousy cartographers.

(A cartographer is a person who makes maps. I'm not sure why a person who makes maps gets such a fancy name, while people who make things like bread or metal objects or dinner get more humdrum names like baker, smith, and cook. Perhaps it's because cartographers need to be really good at their jobs. If a baker makes a mistake, you only get lousy bread, and if a smith makes a mistake, you only get a crummy sword, and if a cook makes a bad dinner, you get indigestion. But if a cartographer makes a mistake, you end up sailing off the edge of the world. Or not realizing that there's more than one kraken.)

Obviously, the squid should have written "krakens"

on the map, with an *s*. Not just "kraken."

There are a few reasons they might have gotten this wrong:

1) As Princess Piscina had pointed out, squid have terrible handwriting. In fact, they don't even have hands, which might be the root of the problem.

2) Squid don't understand plurals very well. After all, the plural of "squid" is "squid," which is obviously just wrong.

3) Squid are idiots.

Whatever the case, the word "kraken" on the map had led us to believe there was only a single kraken. So when the first kraken (which was just a little kraken) swam away so quickly, it didn't occur to any of us that there might be another kraken around.

And it certainly didn't occur to us that this other kraken might be absolutely massive.

The kraken was also surprisingly quiet for something the size of a small kingdom. So we didn't notice it right away. We just sat there, staring off in the direction that the little kraken had gone, foolishly thinking that we were the ones who had frightened it off.

"I'm surprised all that shouting worked," Belinda said.

"Me too," I agreed. "Maybe the kraken is just very sensitive to loud noises."

"It probably doesn't hear much shouting, living underwater," Princess Grace added thoughtfully. "I don't think fish or shrimp or other sea creatures can shout, can they?"

"Fish certainly can't," Ferkle said. "I did a whole report on it in Village Idiot School. I spent two weeks insulting all sorts of different sea creatures, and not a single one shouted back at me."

"There's a Village Idiot School?" I asked.

"Oh yes," Ferkle replied. "You can't just decide to be a village idiot. Even if the profession runs in your family, you have to train for it. There are courses on how to properly fall down in a patch of mud, and how to make funny noises with different parts of your body, and what types of vegetables you can shove up your nose and . . . Does anyone have the sense that something is watching us?"

Belinda said, "Now that you mention it, I do. I wonder why that is?"

"I think it's because something *is* watching us," said Princess Grace, who had finally turned around and noticed the kraken. Then she screamed at the top of her lungs.

The rest of us turned around and saw the kraken as well.

Then we screamed at the top of our lungs.

The seahorses also saw the kraken.

They whinnied in terror and began swimming as fast as they could.

There is a lot of debate about what the fastest sea creature is. Some people say it is the sailfish. Some say it is the speed-shark. Some say it is a goldfish that has been dropped from a very great height. But I know from experience that the fastest sea creatures are a pair of seahorses that have just noticed that the world's biggest kraken is directly behind them.

I am aware that a few pages back, I said the seahorses were exhausted. Well, faced with the giant kraken, they suddenly

found some reserves of energy. They took off so quickly that
we were all thrown off our feet and tumbled into the back of
the rowboat. Then they rocketed away, dragging us behind
them at a rate so fast that we had to hold on to the sides of
the boat to keep from being blown overboard.

This sudden burst of speed caught the kraken by surprise. It took a moment for it to realize what had happened; then it dove underwater and vanished from sight.

"Hmmm," Princess Grace mused. "Do you think we
scared that one away too?"

"I don't think so," Belinda said, watching the water
behind us with concern.

A great, dark, exceptionally ugly shadow was quickly
growing bigger below the surface.

Then the kraken exploded out of the water and flew
through the air toward us, its massive, toothy mouth wide
open.

Even though they had already broken the record for
fastest-swimming sea creature, our seahorses decided to go
even faster. Now we were moving at such great speed that
the rowboat was skipping across the surface of the water like
a thrown stone.

This burst of speed kept us just out of range of the kraken, which plunged back down into the sea behind us.

That was the good news.

The bad news was that the impact of the kraken in the sea created an absolutely enormous wave, which swept us up and lifted us high into the sky.

THE QUEST OF DANGER

We now found ourselves sledding quickly down the front slope of a mountain of water. We overtook our exhausted seahorses, which fell into the rowboat with us, knocking Princess Grace backward. She nearly toppled off the stern of the rowboat, but Belinda lunged and grabbed her arm at the last second, pulling her to safety.

Well, maybe "safety" isn't the best way to describe a tiny rowboat on the flank of a tsunami. But Princess Grace's chances of survival improved from 0 to about 1 percent.

The huge wave was moving even faster than the seahorses had swum, carrying us away from the kraken and toward land. As it reached shallower water, it got smaller but still kept moving. We were carried over coral reefs and the beach, and then the foamy crest of the wave broke above us. The rowboat splintered into pieces, and we all found ourselves tumbling head over heels through the water.

I had no idea which way was up or down or where any of my friends were. All I knew was that I was wet and dizzy and had no air to breathe.

Then the wave came apart. We had reached land, and I wound up splayed out in a field, gasping for breath

among a great number of very startled sea creatures.
Flustered flounders flopped in the grass. Outraged octopuses dangled from the trees. A startled swordfish was
embedded nose-first in the ground, like a giant dart.

I heard sputtering and coughing around me. I sat up
and saw Ferkle with his head stuck in a giant clam.

Rover was chasing a catfish, looking completely fine.

The seahorses were in a small lagoon, exhausted but alive.

The kraken was way off in the sea, looking very disappointed about losing its dinner. We were too far inland for it to get to us, so it grumbled angrily and then sank back into the water.

Belinda and Princess Grace lay in the sand nearby, wet and bedraggled ◁ IQ BOOSTER! ▷ but otherwise all right.

("Bedraggled" means "dirty, muddy, soiled, unkempt, and generally untidy.")

In fact, Princess Grace was looking at Belinda with a kind of dreamy gaze. "You saved me!" she said, fluttering her eyelashes.

And then the cyclops attacked.

CHAPTER SEVEN

Why the Cyclops Was So Angry

My parents had also told me scary tales about the cyclops, just in case the ones about the kraken hadn't scared me into behaving.

A cyclops is a giant with only one eye, which is smack in the middle of its forehead. They are famous for their foul tempers and their habit of smashing people with large objects. Cyclopes do not like people on normal days, but this day was worse than normal, because of the tsunami that had just swamped their land.

"Somebody flooded all my fields!" the cyclops roared. His voice was loud and resonant. **← IQ BOOSTER !**

("Resonant" means "deep, clear, and continuing to ring." The cyclops's voice was so resonant, it made my bones vibrate. I felt like a plucked guitar string.)

We all turned around to see the cyclops standing on a hill behind us, holding an enormous club made from an entire tree trunk, looking over the land with a great frown on his face.

"And somebody got fish all over the place!" the cyclops continued, sounding even more annoyed. "Ick! I *hate* fish! Who did this?"

Ferkle, Belinda, Princess Grace, and I all did our best to look inconspicuous. ⊲ ANOTHER IQ BOOSTER!

("Inconspicuous" means "not clearly visible or attracting attention." Have you ever done something you knew was wrong, like breaking a precious family heirloom? And you knew your parents (or Grandpa Joe or Great-Aunt Franny) would be upset, so you did your best to pretend that you had nothing to do with it, hoping that maybe they would think your brother or sister or dog was responsible? Well, that's what we tried to do right then.)

We looked off into the distance and twiddled our thumbs and acted innocent, hoping that the cyclops would not notice us.

To our surprise, it seemed to work. The cyclops didn't spot us. Although that might not have been due to our fine acting skills. There seemed to be something wrong with his vision. He was squinting at the landscape and frowning, as though he sensed we were there but couldn't see us.

"Is someone here?" the cyclops yelled.

None of us said a thing. We didn't even breathe. We just stayed still and hoped the cyclops wouldn't notice us.

Which might have worked if Rover hadn't started barking.

It wasn't just a little bark. He ran directly toward the cyclops, barking as loud as he could, and wouldn't stop.

"He's going to get us in trouble!" Belinda exclaimed. "What on earth is that stupid fr-dog thinking?"

"I never know," I said.

What Rover Was Thinking

Dum de dum de dum. Doo be doo be doo. Dum de dum de dum. Doo be doo be doo. Dum de dum de dum. Doo be doo be doo. Dum de dum de dum. Doo be doo be doo. Dum de dum de dum. Doo be doo be doo. Dum de dum de dum. Doo be doo be doo. Dum de dum de dum. Doo be doo be doo. Doo be doo be doo. Dum de dum de dum. Doo be doo be doo. Dum de dum de dum. Doo be doo be doo. Dum de dum de dum. Doo be doo be doo. Dum de dum de dum. Doo be doo be doo. Dum de dum de dum. Doo be doo be doo. Dum de dum de dum. Doo be doo be doo. Dum de dum de dum. Doo be doo be doo. Dum de dum de dum. Doo be doo be doo. Dum de dum de dum. Doo be doo be doo. Dum de dum de dum. Dum de dum de . . .

Hey! That guy has a stick! The biggest stick I've ever seen! Maybe, if I bark really loudly, he'll throw the stick, and then I can fetch it! Fetching sticks is the best thing ever!

Hey, giant one-eyed guy! Throw the stick! Throw the stick! THROW THE STICK!!!!

Oh! He's going to throw it! Hooray! I love fetch!!!!

CHAPTER EIGHT

How We Got Away

The cyclops was not happy to see Rover barking at him. He lifted his giant club, ready to smash my fr-dog.

I cringed, worried this would be the end of Rover.

The cyclops brought the club down on the ground so hard that all the fish strewn around bounced into the air.

Thankfully, he didn't hit Rover. In fact, he missed by a great deal.

Rover kept barking, not realizing that the cyclops was trying to kill him!

The cyclops tried to clobber him again.

Once again, he pounded the earth so hard that all the fish bounced into the air.

And once again, he wasn't anywhere close to Rover.

Belinda was the first to grasp why this had happened. "He can barely see!" she exclaimed.

"Of course!" Ferkle cried. "He only has one eye! So he has terrible depth perception!" IQ BOOSTER!

(This isn't a definition so much as an interesting scientific fact: depth perception is the ability to perceive the relative distance of objects. Humans tend to have rather good depth perception, because we have two eyes, both of which look forward. Animals with eyes on the sides of their head, like horses and dragons and bargleboars, do not have very good depth perception. And neither do cyclopes, because they only have one eye. You'd think that this would be mentioned more in stories of courageous knights who fought cyclopes, but I suppose those knights left this part out, thinking that they would seem less courageous if everyone knew they were fighting an enemy who was completely incapable of hitting their target.)

The cyclops tried to hit Rover again and again. He missed every time.

"I think he might be slightly myopic, ⟨ IQ BOOSTER! too," Ferkle observed.

("Myopic" is a fancy term for being nearsighted, meaning that the cyclops couldn't see anything unless it was close to his eye. And when you are several stories tall, *nothing* is close to your eye. Basically, this cyclops needed glasses. Or a monocle, I suppose, which is a glass for only one eye.)

The cyclops might not have been able to see Rover, but he could still *hear* Rover, because my fr-dog was barking continuously. The cyclops was obviously growing more and more frustrated with his failure to smash the little barking thing, so he finally flung his club, hoping that might do the trick.

Instead, the club missed Rover by a great distance and plopped into a bog far away.

Rover ran off to fetch it.

"Rover!" Princess Grace yelled. "Come back!"

This was not a good idea. The cyclops heard her shout, turned our way, and actually managed to spot us.

"People!" he exclaimed. "I knew it! You're the ones who flooded my fields!"

Since he no longer had a club, he grabbed some boulders off the ground and started throwing them at us.

But since he had no depth perception (and was possibly myopic), they missed us by a mile.

Literally. All of them landed a mile away from us.

We ran anyhow.

There was no point in staying close to a cyclops who was trying to crush us with stones. Even one with lousy aim. Sooner or later, he still might hit us.

Rover recovered the club and bounded after us with it clenched in his jaws.

The cyclops's vision might not have been that good, but he could see well enough to know we were running away (although we probably looked like fuzzy blurs to him).

He raced after us, yelling angrily. "Come back here, you darn field-flooders! You and your little green barking thing are in a lot of trouble! I'll smash you to smithereens! I'll bash you to bits! I'll crush you into . . . Whoa!!!"

That "whoa" was not a shout of anger. It was a cry of surprise.

Even though I really needed to focus on running away, I turned back to see what had happened.

Behind me, Rover still seemed to be thinking that he was playing fetch with the cyclops. He had brought the giant stick back to him and dropped it at his feet.

And then the cyclops, having bad depth percep-tion (and possibly myopia) had failed to notice it. So this happened:

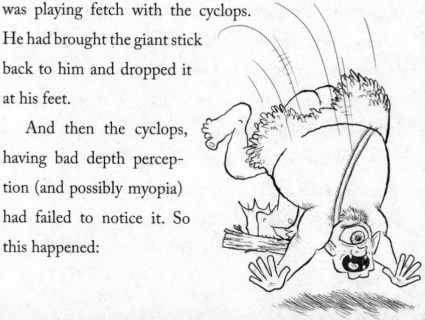

Now, instead of running after us, the cyclops was flying through the air toward us, his arms pinwheeling wildly.

"Look out!" I yelled.

Everyone scrambled out of the way as the cyclops crashed to the ground and tumbled past us. He slammed headfirst into some rocks by the shore, hitting them so hard that they cracked apart.

I thought he might have been knocked unconscious, but then he sat up, looking very upset.

"I've got something in my eye!" he wailed, and then rubbed it furiously with one of his enormous fists.

I have gotten something in my eye before. It was annoying, but I was able to still function, because I had another eye that was working just fine.

That was not the case with the cyclops.

Also, when I got something in my eye, it was very tiny, like a piece of dirt or a gnat.

But the cyclops was enormous, and the thing he had gotten stuck in his eye was a wayward octopus that had been thrown ashore by the tsunami.

"It hurts!" the cyclops wailed. "It hurts! Help me get it out!"

We did not help him. Because we feared that, being a cyclops, he would try to harm us the moment he could see again.

Instead, we quickly slipped away and scurried across the countryside, escaping as fast as we could.

We could still hear the cyclops wailing in the distance as we fled.

"Ow ow ow!" he cried. "It hurts!"

"That cyclops is having a pretty bad day," Princess Grace noted.

"Not nearly as bad a day as that octopus, though," Ferkle replied.

We all had to admit that was probably true.

Of course, we weren't having that good a day either.

And it only got worse when we reached Atlantis.

CHAPTER NINE

What Atlantis Was Like

It took us a while to get to Atlantis. We had no ships to sail along the coast or horses to carry us across the land. Instead, we had to walk the whole way, which was very little fun, because our shoes were wet and squelchy, and our clothes were also wet and chafed our buttocks. And also, our rock map from Merland weighed as much as a pregnant goat, so we each had to take turns carrying it. We walked for the

entire rest of the day and then camped for the night, eating nuts and berries that we found along the way.

The next morning, we finally reached our destination.

It was the most amazing place I had ever seen.

Although, I must admit that, up until that time, I hadn't seen very many places, and most of those were rather crummy. In the village where I had spent nearly my entire life, every building except the castle was made out of mud. There was only one road (which was also made of mud), a single well, and no sewers; everyone just did their business in a chamber pot which they then emptied out the window. It was a dull, dreary, dirty, extremely smelly place—and yet, it was still regarded as one of the nicer villages in the kingdom.

Since becoming a knight, I had visited some other places and had not been impressed. Most looked almost exactly the same as my home village, only with more dragons or extra plague. I will admit, a few locations had been somewhat beautiful, but they were still full of vicious beasts or evil people who were trying to kill me.

On the other hand, Atlantis was really quite stunning.
I mean, look at it:

It was located on a beautiful harbor. It had a nice, sturdy
wall to keep out dragons and bargleboars and hordes of
vicious invaders. The homes and shops were made out of
stone—and some of them were over one story tall! Even
from a distance, we could tell it had a sewer system; it didn't
reek of used chamber pots. Instead, it smelled delightful,

like fresh flowers and fruit and roasted meat.

It also appeared to be extremely safe. I knew this because of the sign out front:

I realize that seventeen years might not seem like a terribly long time to go without a major disaster of some sort, but back in my time, a village was usually lucky to go a few days without burning down or being invaded by orcs or having a basilisk infestation. So Atlantis's long stretch without trouble seemed incredible to all of us.

"Seventeen years!" Princess Grace exclaimed. "This must be the safest city of all time!"

"Yes," Belinda said. "Although . . . do you think that's because they've just had a spell of good luck? If so, perhaps they're due for a major disaster."

"I doubt it," Ferkle assured her. "Atlantis is so safe because the architects have taken great care to build it well, with strong buildings and dragon-proof walls. I wouldn't be surprised if this city remained standing for centuries to come."

"Wow," I said, impressed. Since Ferkle was the smartest of us, I was extremely comforted by his words. Atlantis seemed like an even better place than it had just moments before.

The only bad part was the black ship in the harbor.

It was docked alongside several other ships, some of which were for merchants, and some of which were for the Atlantis navy. Every inch of the ship was black, from the bow to the stern, even the sails.

It was the same ship that Prince Ruprecht and his band of pirates had ambushed us from. Which meant that

Ruprecht, his pirates, and the elder knights who had aban-
doned us to join forces with the enemy were all in Atlantis.

The ship was
crawling with pirates.

"There's no way we're getting past all of those evildoers,"
Belinda said disappointedly. "If the trident and all the other
treasures are still aboard, we'll never be able to get them."

"I doubt Ruprecht left all the treasures there," Ferkle
said wisely. "He would never trust a band of pirates to
guard them. He must still have the treasures with him."

"But then where is he?" I asked.

"We'll have to do some snooping around to find out," Ferkle replied. Then he scooped up a handful of mud and smashed it into his face.

I sighed. "You don't have to pretend to be the village idiot everywhere we go. We're nowhere near our village anymore."

"First of all, being the village idiot is my *job*," Ferkle said, sounding as though I had insulted his honor. "Just like being a knight is your job. You have sworn to protect the princess, and I have sworn to be an idiot. Second, to find out what Ruprecht is up to, we are going to have to be very sneaky. Being a village idiot is a great way to do that. No one pays any attention to the village idiot. And no one ever expects you to be plotting something clever when you are wearing a live chicken on your head."

"Ah," Belinda said, impressed. "I see! That's a brilliant plan!" Then she found some mud and smashed it into her face as well.

Princess Grace observed this with obvious disgust. "Are we *sure* it's brilliant?" she asked warily. "Isn't there some way of getting into the city that doesn't involve being filthy?"

"You're *already* filthy," I pointed out.

"I know," Princess Grace said sourly. All of us were grimy and bedraggled from our adventures. "But I was hoping to find a place to get *less* dirty here. Atlantis is famed for three things: being completely disaster-proof, its fine sewer systems—and its public baths. I *soooo* want to visit the public baths. I could really use a good scrubbing."

"Perhaps you could go later," Belinda told her. "I know that being dirty isn't fun for you, but at the moment, it's necessary to achieve our objectives."

Princess Grace looked into Belinda's eyes and softened. "You're right as usual, Bull," she said, fluttering her eyelashes again. "You're very smart."

The way Princess Grace was looking at Belinda really worried me. It made me realize that, sooner or later, I would to have to tell Princess Grace the truth about Belinda, which was going to be a problem.

But this was not the time. We had work to do.

Ferkle gave us a quick lesson in village idiocy, teaching us how to make dumb faces and create silly noises with various parts of our bodies. Then we disguised ourselves.

Belinda coated herself with extra mud and chicken feathers. Princess Grace stuck leaves and bits of broccoli in her hair. I put my pants on backward and found a passing hamster to use as a hat.

However, I had to tie Rover up outside the city, because, as the only fr-dog on the planet, he was rather noticeable.

I found him a nice place beside a brook with fresh water and lots of shade. He immediately curled up and went to sleep.

Then we headed into Atlantis.

Ferkle was right. People saw us, but they didn't really *look* at us. Instead, they avoided us, as though fearful that

idiocy was contagious. They moved to the other side of the street and gave us a wide berth as we passed.

We walked right by the harbor, including Ruprecht's black ship with all the pirates. None of them paid any attention to us.

Atlantis had large and imposing front gates that were patrolled by armed guards, but the gates were open during the day to allow merchants and tradesmen through, and while the guards noticed us, they weren't the slightest bit suspicious. Instead, they laughed as we went by.

"Looks like the idiot patrol is here," one chuckled.

"Dum de dum de dum," said Ferkle, and then walked into a gatepost for good measure.

The guards went right back to their conversation and forgot all about us.

We moved through the city with ease.

On the other hand, I couldn't help but stare at *everything*. Atlantis was even more impressive close-up. I mean, look at it!

There were grand plazas with burbling fountains and beautiful statues, groups of minstrels playing lovely

music, and markets that sold food that wasn't gruel: fruit, bread, and grilled meats, as well as foreign delicacies I had never even seen before. (Including a bizarre substance called cheese that was made from moldy dairy products and smelled like feet; I stayed away from it, although the Atlanteans appeared to think it was very tasty.)

"This city is gorgeous," I said quietly to my friends, so that no one else would hear.

"And extremely well built," Ferkle added, tapping a stone building as we passed. "I'm now absolutely positive that no terrible disasters could ever possibly befall this place. I'll bet that, many centuries in the future, everyone will regard Atlantis as the safest city ever built!"

The rest of us nodded in agreement, unaware of the dramatic irony ⟨ IQ BOOSTER! ⟩ of Ferkle's statement.

(Dramatic irony is a clever literary technique occasionally employed by very talented authors in which the audience—which would be you, in this case—knows something that the characters do not. Like what Atlantis is actually famous for in the future. This is not to be confused with dramatic ironing, which is the process of pressing one's clothes so that they look really fantastic.)

We continued on through Atlantis, passing the public baths. There were two large, wonderfully decorated buildings, from which Atlanteans were emerging, looking very odd.

"What's wrong with those people?" Belinda asked.

"They're *clean*," Princess Grace said, sounding extremely jealous. "That's what you look like when you don't have years' worth of dirt caked all over your body."

"They seem very happy about it," Belinda observed.

"Yes, I'm sure they are," Princess Grace said. "I don't suppose I could stop in there for a quick shower and a loofa rub? I promise I'll be out by sunset."

"No," Belinda told her firmly. "We have to focus on our mission."

"I suppose you're right," Princess Grace admitted. "You really are very smart and dedicated, Bull." Then she gave Belinda another one of her besotted ⟨ IQ BOOSTER! ⟩ looks.

("Besotted" means "seriously lovestruck." This was becoming way more than just a little crush.)

I groaned, reminded once again that I was going to have to figure out how to deal with this.

But before I could, we ran into Prince Ruprecht.

CHAPTER TEN

What Prince Ruprecht Was Up To

Ruprecht was not alone. He was with his entire retinue. (As you may recall, I defined this word in the last book. But in case you forgot, a retinue is a group of advisers and assistants who accompany an important person. Retinues were quite common in my time, as every person who was important—or who *thought* they were important—had one.)

Ruprecht's retinue consisted of:

1) Nerlim, his wicked adviser. Nerlim claimed to be a wizard, although he was not very good at it. However, he *was* very good at coming up with evil plans, which was why Ruprecht kept him around.

2) The elder knights of Merryland. Only a few days before, they had been our mentors, but they had opted to

switch sides and work with Ruprecht because Ruprecht had treasure and was threatening to kill them. The knights consisted of Sir Vyval the Brave; Sir Vaylance the Observant; Sir Cumference the Rotund; Sir Fass the Dim-Witted; Sir Cuss the Crotchety; Sir Mount, the One with a Horse; Sir Mount's horse, the Steed; and the stableman formerly known as Sir Render the Cowardly.

3) A random assortment of pirates. I didn't really know these pirates, as the only time I had met them was when they were tying me up and sending me off in a rowboat toward the edge of the world, but from that behavior, I could presume that they were a bunch of jerks.

Ruprecht was wearing much of the treasure that he had stolen. He had the Mystical Protective Amulet of Merryland on a gold chain around his neck, the Golden Crown of Tinkerdink perched on his head, the Royal Robes of Roobadoob around his shoulders, and many jeweled rings on his fingers. Meanwhile, the knights carried golden scepters and staffs and orbs—and the Great Trident of Merland.

With all his stolen treasure and his large retinue,

Sir Vaylance

Prince Ruprecht

Pirate

Sir Cumference

Sir Render

Sir Cuss

Sir Mount

Sir Vyval

Nerlim

Sir Fass

Another pirate

And another pirate

Ruprecht looked very rich and powerful and important. All the Atlanteans stared at him with awe and respect.

That meant no one was looking at *us*. Ruprecht certainly wasn't, because we looked like a bunch of fools.

No one else in his retinue noticed us either, except for

Nerlim, who only gave us a cursory [IQ BOOSTER!] glance and then moved on.

("Cursory" means "very brief," like this definition.)

Nerlim did not recognize us. But then he probably did not expect us to be posing as idiots, and he certainly didn't expect that we would have somehow survived our trip over the edge of the earth, allied ourselves with the merpeople, and made it to Atlantis.

Prince Ruprecht and his retinue continued past us and headed up to the castle.

We followed him to see what he was up to.

Lots of Atlanteans followed him as well, fascinated by this rich and powerful and important prince.

The castle was the most impressive building in all Atlantis, which was really saying something.

It was the tallest building I had ever seen, with some turrets that were a whole five stories in height. It was built from shiny white stone and covered with beautiful carvings of maidens and angels. Even within the safety of the city, it still had additional protective measures. There was a moat full of sharks and a drawbridge patrolled by even more guards.

"Halt!" the first guard yelled. "Who goes there?"

Nerlim stepped forward and announced, "This is the rich and powerful and important Prince Ruprecht of the Kingdom of Wyld. He has been summoned to the castle by the king and queen of Atlantis, who are looking for someone rich and powerful and important to seek the hand of their daughter, Princess Petunia!"

And just like that, my friends and I realized what Ruprecht's evil plan was.

"He's using the stolen treasure to make himself look rich and powerful and important!" I exclaimed.

"Which he needs to do because the king and queen of Wyld spent all the kingdom's money," Ferkle added.

"And once he marries Princess Petunia," Belinda went on, "then he'll become part of the richest and most powerful kingdom in the land. And once a no-good bully like that has money and power and an army, then he'll be really, really dangerous."

Princess Grace looked at her, impressed. "You are sooo smart," she said.

"Thanks," Belinda said. "We need to figure out some

way to get word to the king and queen of Atlantis that Ruprecht can't be trusted."

Princess Grace suddenly lit up with excitement. "I know how to do that!" she announced. "And even better . . . it's going to require a bath!"

CHAPTER ELEVEN

What Princess Grace's Plan Was

"If you want to talk to a king or a queen," Princess Grace explained as she hurried us back through Atlantis, "then you have to appear rich and powerful and important. Royal people don't like to talk to anyone except other royal people."

"*You* talk to other people," I reminded her.

"Yes, but I'm special," Princess Grace said. "And right now, even though I *am* royalty, I don't *look* like royalty. I look like a village idiot. If I say I'm a princess, no one will ever believe me. Which is where the baths come in. I need to get cleaned and scrubbed and perfumed so that I am believable."

"This plan sounds like a ruse to go to the baths," I whispered to Ferkle.

"Perhaps," he replied, "but there is also some sense to it."

The baths were not free, but it turned out that Princess Grace had a gold coin sewed into the hem of her clothes for emergencies. "I can't think of a bigger emergency than this," she said, and then paid for the four of us to enter.

I will admit, I was very skeptical ◁ IQ BOOSTER! of Princess Grace's plan.

("Skeptical" means "having doubts" and "not easily convinced." For example, a curmudgeonly teacher might be skeptical that this book is educational—until you reveal that you have learned what "skeptical" means from reading it.)

I wasn't sure this plan would work, and I was very wary of baths. I'd had baths before. Three of them, in fact. They had all involved extremely cold water and very scratchy sponges.

It turns out, the baths in Atlantis were quite different.

Each bath was private (which was good news for Belinda). The water was nice and warm. The sponges were soft. The soap smelled delightful. There were even little jets that directed streams of water to massage your back and shoulders.

A normal bath:

A bath in Atlantis:

Now I understood why Princess Grace had been so excited to bathe. Some of the dirt and grime on my body had been there so long, it felt like it was a part of me. (I'm quite sure that there were patches of gunk behind each of my ears that had been there since shortly after I was born.) But now I was actually *clean*. I felt fantastic—and possibly a few pounds lighter. My skin tingled all over. I didn't want to ever get back out of the tub again.

But I had to. Duty called. And besides, Princess Grace had another surprise waiting.

She had bought us new clothes.

I had never owned new clothes before. The clothes I had been wearing had been handed down through my family for generations. They were itchy and scratchy and smelled like the body odor of three dozen people. Princess Grace had arranged for my old clothes to be burned, then buried, and then had the burial site set on fire for good measure.

Wearing new clothes felt even better than being clean. Unlike my old hand-me-downs, they were soft and comfortable and didn't have large families of lice living in them.

I almost didn't recognize Ferkle or Belinda. I had never seen either of them clean before. (It turned out Ferkle's hair wasn't even dark; it had just been full of dirt and mud.) And they had just as much trouble recognizing me. We stopped and stared at one another for quite a while, stunned by the change.

We had no trouble recognizing Princess Grace, though. We were used to seeing her clean and in fine new clothes (although over the course of our adventures, she had occasionally gotten very dirty). So when she exited the baths, we were not quite as surprised.

What *did* surprise us were how many other people recognized her. Princess Grace was famed throughout the many kingdoms for her beauty. (I know she had lots of other fine qualities, but sadly, back in our day, beauty was pretty much the only thing anyone cared about in a princess.) Random passersby stopped in their tracks to stare in amazement at her, and word quickly spread that Princess Grace from the Kingdom of Merryland was in Atlantis.

Among those who stopped to stare were an entire royal retinue. Prince Schmendrick of Atlantis—the brother of Princess Petunia—happened to be on his way to the baths. Since Atlantis was an extremely rich and powerful city, Prince Schmendrick did not walk through the streets. That was considered too pedestrian. ⟨ IQ BOOSTER!

("Pedestrian" means "dull" or "common"—and it also

means "a person who is walking." So really, both defini-
tions of the word work in this case, which makes the use
of it in this context extremely
clever, if I do say so myself.)

Riding a horse was
also considered beneath
Schmendrick's status. In
fact, Schmendrick was
so fancy, even his horse
didn't walk through
the streets. Instead,
Schmendrick was
seated on a large
throne, which
was carried on the
shoulders of his
servants. And then
his horse was carried on a much larger
throne on the shoulders of a group of far
more unfortunate servants.

Prince Schmendrick did not understand

why his retinue had stopped at first. He was too busy eating peeled grapes that were being fed to him by yet more servants. "Why have we stopped, you fools?" he demanded angrily. "You know I am in desperate need of a bath! I have a smudge of dirt on my left elbow that is extremely unsightly! Now make haste or else I shall have all of you thrown in the dungeon—"

At this point, his gaze fell upon the reason his reti-
nue had stopped. He sat up in his throne and exclaimed,
"Princess Grace! Holy mackerel! What are you doing in
Atlantis?"

"Hello, Schmendrick," Princess Grace said. "I have
come to warn you of an evil plot. You see, Prince Ruprecht,
who seeks the hand of your sister in marriage, is—"

"Speaking of marriage," Schmendrick interrupted, as
though he hadn't been paying much attention to what
Princess Grace was saying, "you are the most beautiful
woman that I have ever laid eyes upon. And since I happen to be exceedingly handsome, it makes good sense that
we should be married as well."

"What?" Princess Grace asked, thrown by the statement. "First of all, the fact that both of us are extremely
attractive is no basis for a lasting, healthy relationship—"

"Ah, I suppose you're right," Schmendrick said. "There's
also that fact that I am very rich. That makes me the perfect catch. So, how's tomorrow afternoon for the wedding?"

Now Princess Grace was horrified. "I'm not going to
marry you tomorrow afternoon! Or ever! You are vain and

mean to your servants! I wouldn't marry you if you were the richest man on earth!"

"But I *am* the richest man on earth," Schmendrick said. "So I guess that's settled. Shall we say two o'clock?"

"No!" Princess Grace snapped, exasperated. "I am not interested in a pompous buffoon [DOUBLE IQ BOOSTER!] like you, and I never will be!"

("Pompous" is another word for "vain," while a buffoon is a ridiculous, clownish person. If you put them together, it's quite an insult, which is why all the Atlanteans gasped in shock when Princess Grace said it.)

Schmendrick now grew very embarrassed and upset. "I don't think I want to marry you at all!" he snapped. "You are a nasty girl who has poor manners and a terrible bumbershoot." [IQ BOOSTER!]

(A bumbershoot is an umbrella. Schmendrick obviously did not know what it meant. He was probably trying to sound intelligent after Princess Grace had used some big words herself—which only made him look dumber.)

"A bumbershoot is an umbrella," Princess Grace informed him. "Not only are you pompous and mean, but you are also a dummy. Apparently, I will have to use very small words to explain Ruprecht's plot to you so that you understand me. . . ."

Unfortunately, Schmendrick was now too cross to listen to Princess Grace. (Not that he would have listened to her anyhow.) "*You're* the dummy!" he replied childishly. "I take back what I said about you being beautiful! You're very ugly! The marriage is off! Servants, take me to the baths at once! Talking to this woman has made me feel even dirtier!"

His servants dutifully whisked him away into the baths.

Princess Grace huffed angrily and stormed off through the city.

Belinda, Ferkle, and I raced after her.

"Uh . . . Princess," Ferkle said. "The plan was to inform the royal family about what Ruprecht was up to, not to insult the prince."

"Schmendrick wasn't even going to listen to me!" Princess Grace growled. "All he cared about were my looks!"

"I understand he was offensive," Ferkle said, "but you seem to have forgotten about our plan to get the treasures back. Perhaps you could apologize to Schmendrick and then fake interest in his marriage proposal so that he is willing to listen to you. . . ."

"Apologize to that jerk?" Princess Grace exclaimed. "And then fake interest in him? No way! I couldn't possibly even *think* about marrying a jackaninny like that! If I ever have a loving relationship, it will be with someone who is smart and brave and kind and selfless. . . ." As she said this, she stole a glance at Belinda and turned slightly red from embarrassment.

I realized that Belinda was the person she was describing and grew worried once again.

Princess Grace had just rejected the richest and most eligible prince on earth and was pining away for someone she did not know the whole truth about. This was getting to be a very big problem. I knew I couldn't let Princess Grace go on like this for much longer. I was going to have to betray Belinda's trust and tell Princess Grace the facts about Belinda.

But before I could, we were captured.

CHAPTER TWELVE

Who Had Captured Us This Time

Everything happened very fast.

One moment, we were walking along the streets of Atlantis, and the next, someone had grabbed each of us and stuffed us in sacks. Then we were carried roughly through the city. We didn't even know who had grabbed us until we were dumped back out of the sacks again and found ourselves in the hold of a ship, facing a woman dressed like this:

As you can see, there were several pirates around her.

I recognized some of them from the black ship that Prince Ruprecht had been on when he ambushed us, and so I assumed that we were in the hold of that very ship. But the woman was unfamiliar to me.

"The four of you are obviously far more clever than I realized," the woman said.

"Who are you?" Belinda asked.

"My name is Calliope," she replied. "And I am the pirate queen."

Princess Grace considered her from head to toe. "You don't *look* like a pirate. Pirates have hooks and eye patches and peg legs and parrots. And you don't sound like a pirate either. Pirates speak with bad grammar and say 'arrrr' a lot."

"That is an offensive stereotype," Calliope replied. "There are many, many pirates who avoid injury, dislike parrots, and speak in an erudite ⟨ IQ BOOSTER! ⟩ manner."

("Erudite" means "showing great knowledge or learning." In using the word "erudite," Calliope was showing us how erudite she was.)

"That's right, Queen Calliope!" a pirate by her side agreed. "We pirates be very erudite. Arrrr!"

"Arrrr!" agreed all the other pirates.

Calliope smacked her face with her hand, then wheeled on the pirates. "Quiet!" she shouted. "You're embarrassing me!"

The pirates instantly fell silent and looked ashamed.

Calliope returned her attention to us. "As I was saying, you are obviously very clever. You not only managed to escape death at the falls, but you also figured out where we were heading, got here quickly, and would have ruined our plans if Prince Schmendrick hadn't been too foolish to listen to you. Therefore, the next time we arrange for a way to kill you, we will have to stick around and make sure it works."

"Or how about this?" Belinda suggested. "You could *not* kill us and join forces with us against Ruprecht."

Calliope laughed. "You are not only clever. You are also audacious."  IQ BOOSTER!

("Audacious" means "surprisingly bold" and also "showing a lack of respect."

I'm not quite sure which definition Calliope was using. Both would have worked.)

"Why would I join forces with you?" Calliope continued. "You have nothing to bargain with and are at my mercy, while Prince Ruprecht is going to make us rich."

"How's that?" Belinda asked.

Calliope explained. "Once he wins the hand of Princess Petunia and gains his share of the wealth of Atlantis, he will reward us with great riches for our help."

"Great riches!" the pirates exclaimed. "Arrrr!"

Calliope glowered at them again. "The next one of you who says 'arrr' gets thrown to the sharks."

The pirates all clammed up.

Meanwhile, I saw a chance to get away. It was a slim chance, but it was also the only thing I could come up with.

"That sounds like a very nice plan," I said. "But there's just one problem with it: it won't work."

Calliope looked at me curiously. "And why is that?"

"Because you can't trust Prince Ruprecht," I told her. "He is greedy and dishonest, and he will double-cross you the moment he gets the chance. He'll get rich, and you'll probably all get tossed into the dungeon. Or fed to a dragon. Or something awful like that."

Calliope laughed again. "He would never treat us in such a way. We're a team."

"*We* were his team once," I said. "He brought Bull, Ferkle, and me along to rescue Princess Grace from a stinx. And then, after we helped him do it, he tried to kill us so that we couldn't tell anyone that we'd done all the work."

"That's right!" Princess Grace agreed. "And he is still so angry at us that he has kept trying to kill us over and over again!"

Calliope suddenly didn't look so sure of herself anymore. "You're lying," she said. "You're trying to trick me into turning on Ruprecht."

"Ruprecht has certainly already turned on *you*," Ferkle said. "He turns on everyone who helps him."

"Ha!" Calliope cried. "Now I know you're lying! If Ruprecht turns on *everyone* who helps him, then why hasn't he turned on Nerlim?"

"Because Nerlim is the brains of the operation," I explained.

"That's right," Belinda chimed in. "Nerlim figures out who to double-cross, and then Ruprecht does it. Nerlim is evil, vile, awful, and despicable."

"I'm also right behind you," said Nerlim.

We all wheeled around to find Nerlim standing there. The elder knights of Merryland were arrayed behind him, pointing swords at us.

Nerlim turned to Calliope. "Thanks for capturing these scoundrels. If they had told the Atlanteans our plan, there would be no riches for us to share. I will make sure that you get an even greater portion of the wealth than we promised you before."

Calliope grinned. "Thank you, Nerlim."

Nerlim returned his attention to us. "And as for the four of you, this time, I have a plan guaranteed to make sure you never cause us any more trouble again."

"What's that?" Princess Grace asked. "Are you going to kill us?"

"Worse," Nerlim replied. "I'm giving you jobs in show business."

CHAPTER THIRTEEN

Why Show Business Was So Dangerous

Nerlim and the knights led us to a large arena in the center of Atlantis. It looked like this:

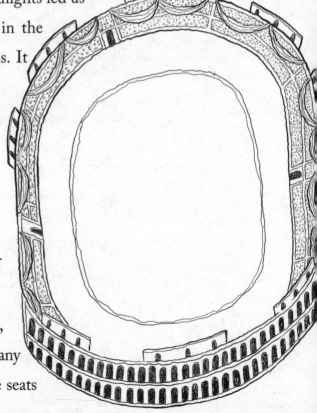

We passed through a dark stone tunnel in the side of it and emerged into the center of the arena. This was a great oval, surrounded by many tiers of seats. The seats were filled with people: more people than I had ever seen in one place in my entire life. In fact, up until that point, I hadn't realized there were that many people on earth. Far more people were gathered in the stands than in the kingdoms of Merryland, Wyld, Tinkerdink, and Dinkum combined.

The people were all very excited. They were dressed festively and waving banners and pennants.

My friends and I were awed and confused.

"What are all these people here for?" I asked.

"They're here to watch sports," Nerlim replied with a smirk.

"What are sports?" Belinda asked.

Sports had not yet been invented in most of the world. When you spent the entire day toiling at work, there was no time for them. Plus, everyone was too exhausted to run around for fun. So there was no football or basketball or soccer or even track and field—although once, my whole town had been moderately distracted by watching my cousin Dingle get chased by a bargleboar.

Nerlim explained. "Sports are athletic competitions between two teams to see who is better."

"All these people are here just to watch other people compete against each other?" Ferkle asked. As smart as he was, sports were a foreign concept to him, as well. "Why?"

"It's quite amusing," Nerlim replied.

"Ooh!" Princess Grace exclaimed. "I greatly enjoy being amused! Is one of these sporting events going to take place soon?"

"Very, very soon," Nerlim said. Then he and all the knights snickered knowingly.

"Will we be able to watch it?" Princess Grace asked.

"Oh, you'll be extremely close to the action," Nerlim said. He and the knights snickered again.

I suddenly began to feel worried. "Er . . . why are we down here in the middle of the arena instead of in the stands with everyone else?"

"Because you're on one of the teams," Nerlim replied.

"Us?" Belinda asked, concerned. "How can we be a team? We don't even know what the rules are."

"The rules are simple," Nerlim explained. "The other team is going to try to kill you, and you're going to try to stay alive."

"Are we allowed to just ask them not to do it?" I asked hopefully.

Nerlim now guffawed loudly. "You can *try*. But they probably won't understand you."

"Oh!" Princess Grace said excitedly, apparently having missed the part about us getting killed. "Are they from another country?"

"No," Nerlim said. "They are a variety of vicious and bloodthirsty beasts. They have been collected from the far reaches of the earth and not fed for a week so that they are ravenously hungry. And soon, they will be released into the center of this arena with you."

This was all very unsettling. ◁ IQ BOOSTER!

("Unsettling" means "causing anxiety." For example, arriving at school to discover that you have forgotten to study for a history test—or to wear pants—is unsettling. Although trust me, it is nowhere near as unsettling as discovering that you are about to be fed to monsters for entertainment.)

My friends were just as unsettled by this news as I was.

"Hold on now," Belinda said, pointing to the stands. "You're telling me that our lives are about to be placed in great danger—and all those people are fine with that?"

"Oh yes," Nerlim replied. "In fact, they are excited to watch it happen."

Belinda frowned. "Not one of them is going to try to help us survive?"

"Of course not!" Nerlim said. "They're all rooting for the beasts to win."

I took a closer look at the Atlanteans in the stands and now noticed what all the banners and pennants they were waving said.

"What is wrong with these people?" Belinda asked.

I turned to the men who had once been the Knight Brigade of Merryland. "You used to be our mentors. Now you're going to let us be fed to a bunch of vicious beasts?"

"Yes," Sir Vyval replied. "Because if we hadn't switched sides to work for Ruprecht, then *we* would be the ones in danger."

"Plus, he's offered us lots of money," Sir Cuss offered helpfully.

"And gold!" Sir Fass added.

"And jewels!" Sir Vaylance said.

"And pie!" Sir Cumference chimed in.

There was a great blare of trumpets, signaling that the royal family was about to arrive. Everyone in the stadium turned to face the royal box, which was a very fancy set of seats.

The entire royal retinue filed in first: trumpeters and guards and advisers and flag bearers and people who dropped rose petals upon the ground for the royals to walk on.

Then the royals themselves arrived. The king and queen of Atlantis, Prince Schmendrick, and Princess Petunia, who was holding the arm of Prince Ruprecht. Ruprecht was still bedecked in all his stolen booty and clutching the Great Trident of Merland in his hands.

The Royal Announcer stepped forward and addressed us all in a loud but mellifluous ⟨ IQ BOOSTER! ⟩ voice.

("Mellifluous" means "pleasant to hear." The Royal Announcer's voice was really quite lovely to listen to—as opposed to the *words* he was saying, which were terrifying.)

"Hear ye, hear ye!" the Announcer announced. "Welcome to the great arena of Atlantis, the finest arena ever constructed, in the center of the greatest and most sturdily built city in all the world—a city which will no doubt stand for centuries to come and certainly won't have anything terrible happen to it like sinking to the bottom of the sea!"

He paused for a breath, then continued, "We have a very exciting gladiatorial combat planned for you today! First, let's meet the visiting team, from the Kingdom of Merryland: the Stinking Traitors Who Are Plotting Against Atlantis!"

The crowd booed and hissed and threw rotten fruit at us, except for one man in a Traitors shirt who cheered. (In every stadium, there's always one guy who likes to root for the underdogs.)

"And now, the home team!" the Announcer exclaimed. "The Brutal and Barbaric Bloodthirsty Beasts!"

The crowd went wild. They whooped and screamed and waved their banners. Even the king and queen behaved like this. They were really big fans of bloodshed in Atlantis.

And yet, the *truly* scary sound came from underneath the arena itself: the howls and snarls and gnashing teeth of the bloodthirsty beasts themselves.

"They must be caged down there somewhere," Ferkle observed. "And they sound exceptionally hungry."

The noises the beasts made were horrifying. The former knights of Merryland trembled so much that their armor rattled—and they weren't even the ones who were about to be eaten.

"Well, it was nice knowing you," Sir Vyval said to us. "We're going to head to safety now." Then he and the other knights and Nerlim all quickly scrambled for the exits, leaving Princess Grace, Belinda, Ferkle, and me unarmed in the center of the arena, awaiting our doom.

Only, it didn't happen.

Because for once, something good took place.

CHAPTER FOURTEEN

Really? Something Good Actually Happened for Once? What Was It?

Before the bloodthirsty beasts could be released into the arena, another scary sound arose from the stands.

It was the sound of Prince Ruprecht wailing.

"Help me!" he cried. "I've been robbed!"

I looked toward the royal box.

While everyone in the stadium had been distracted by us in the middle of the arena, Calliope and the rest of her pirates had snuck up on Ruprecht and swiped all of his treasures. Now, before my eyes, they grabbed on to the great banners that decorated the arena and swung out from the box, like this:

Then they dropped beside us in the center of the arena.

I have to admit, they looked very cool.

"Thanks for the warning that Ruprecht would betray

us," Calliope said. "And for creating a distraction here. It let *us* betray him first."

"You're welcome," Belinda said. "But . . . you've now put yourselves in grave danger, haven't you?"

"Don't worry," Calliope assured her calmly. "We planned for this."

With that, she lit what looked like a long red candle and tossed it at the gate through which we had entered the arena.

It was *not* a candle, of course. Throwing a candle at a big gate is not much of a plan.

It was a stick of dynamite, which I had never seen before. And so I was very startled when the relatively small object created a HUGE explosion. Afterward, there

was nothing left of the gate but a few burning embers.

The royal guards of Atlantis were all still up in the royal box. And Sir Vyval and the rest of the knights had scrambled into the stands. There was no one to prevent us from running for the exit.

So we ran for the exit.

The fans were very upset about this. They had all come expecting a lot of gore and bloodshed, and now the victims were getting away.

The royal family of Atlantis was also upset. Having a guest of honor robbed in your royal box was very embarrassing. It was the sort of thing that gave royal families a bad reputation.

The royal guards were upset because the pirates had made them look like a bunch of ninnies.

But no one was more upset than Prince Ruprecht. "You're not getting away so easily!" he screamed after us. "You're all going to pay for what you've done to me!

There were several large switches in the royal box with all sorts of warnings on them. They looked like this:

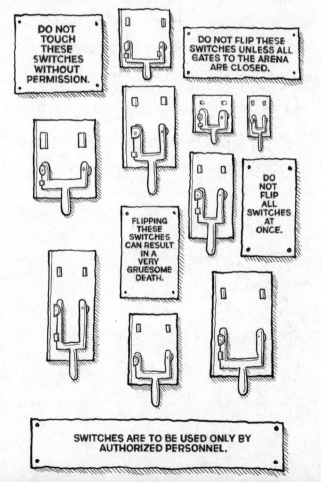

Prince Ruprecht ignored all the warnings and flipped the switches anyhow.

There was a loud, ominous clanking noise from under the arena. It sounded as though lots of heavy machinery had been activated.

Prince Schmendrick wheeled on Prince Ruprecht. "You fool!" he yelled. "Flip them back!"

But it was too late. The switches controlled the intricate series of locks and gates that secured all the vicious and bloodthirsty beasts beneath the arena. And now all these vicious and bloodthirsty beasts—which had been starved for days until they were ravenous—were suddenly released into the arena at once.

The spectators were no longer in a good mood. In fact, they were terrified. Thousands of people fled for the exits at once, fearing that they would be devoured.

However, the beasts decided to go after the closest prey first.

Which was us.

So I suppose that everything didn't work out so well after all.

CHAPTER FIFTEEN

What Happened to Atlantis

There is a riddle from olden times:

What's worse than being chased by one ravenous, bloodthirsty monster?

Being chased by *a lot* of ravenous, bloodthirsty monsters.

I know, it's not that funny. But humor was relatively new in those days, and we were still getting the hang of it. (A few years earlier, Shecky the Hun, the royal jester of the Kingdom of Spatula, had experimented with a gag where he got hit in the face with a cream pie. No one understood why it was supposed to be funny, and then the king of Spatula had him thrown into the dungeon for wasting a perfectly good pie.)

The point is, I had been in many scary situations in

my life so far—and this one was ten times worse than any of them.

The monsters all came after us at once, howling and growling.

We dashed through the hole that Calliope had blown in the side of the arena, escaping into the lovely, clean streets of Atlantis. The streets were nearly empty, as the citizens of Atlantis were all gathered inside the arena to watch us be eaten alive.

A single one of the monsters would have had trouble fitting through the narrow hole. Together, they were much too big— but that didn't stop them from trying. They all piled into the small space at once and then forced their way through it, tearing the foundations

of the arena apart. The enormous, beautiful stadium trembled from the assault—and then began to fall to pieces.

Large chunks of it broke off and slammed into the buildings around it. Then those buildings collapsed and toppled over onto the buildings next to *them*, which toppled onto the next buildings, and so on, as though they were the world's largest set of dominoes.

CRASH!!

Meanwhile, the monsters were still pursuing us through the city, and they weren't showing any more care for the rest of it than they had for the arena. A manticore trampled the central market. A basilisk knocked over the baths. (Which Princess Grace was quite upset about.) An exploding numwrath set the beer-brewing district on fire. (Which all the pirates were *extremely* upset about.)

Of course, the pirates had other things to be concerned about besides the brewery. Running pell-mell through the streets of Atlantis with all the beasts after them would have been difficult enough under normal circumstances, but they were now weighted down with the treasure they had stolen from Ruprecht. All of them were panting and gasping from the exertion. ⟨ IQ BOOSTER!

(Exertion is physical or mental effort. So taking a difficult math test could require a lot of mental exertion, the same way that running for your life from ravenous monsters requires physical exertion. However, if given the choice, I'd pick the math test.)

"Why don't you let me help you carry some of that?" I

offered Calliope. "If you don't give up some of that weight, you'll die."

Calliope actually had to think about this. Because for a pirate, giving up treasure is almost as bad as death.

But then a pursuing bargleboar gnashed its teeth so close to her backside that it took the seat out of her bloomers.

"All right!" she agreed.

I grabbed the Great Trident of Merland from her.

It was much heavier than I had expected. Running with it was a major struggle. I might have simply left it behind if it hadn't been so important to the merpeople.

Plus, I had my own reasons for taking it.

Meanwhile, the monsters were still coming after us and leaving a trail of destruction behind them. They knocked over buildings, clawed up the streets, flattened fountains, and smashed statues.

And as if that wasn't bad enough, Atlantis seemed to be suffering in another way as well. As the monsters stormed through it, the entire city was trembling. It seemed as though its very foundations were being weakened.

We were nearly to the harbor, but it felt as though the city might not even last long enough for us to make it there. More buildings were collapsing. Chasms formed in the streets. And through it all, the monsters kept bearing down on us.

Belinda, Ferkle, and Princess Grace all looked very worried.

"The monsters are almost upon us!" Princess Grace yelled.

"Keep running!" I told her.

"But we're running out of places to run!" Ferkle cried. He pointed ahead of us, to where a good portion of Atlantis had already sunk into the harbor.

"Head into the water!" I said. "I have a plan!"

The others looked at me curiously, although they didn't ask me to elaborate. ◁ IQ BOOSTER !

(To elaborate is to explain something in great detail, which is very hard to do when you are running for your life and gasping for breath and carrying a heavy trident that some merpeople forced you to get for them.)

There was a great rumbling noise from underneath us, followed by an earsplitting crack.

Atlantis fell into the sea.

The waters of the harbor rushed in over the streets— and then the walls and the buildings as they sank beneath the waves. Suddenly we were no longer running. Instead, we were swimming.

The heavy trident nearly dragged me down into the depths, but I held on to it tightly and struggled to stay afloat.

Around me, the pirates were dealing with the same problem. The treasures they were carrying threatened to pull them underwater and drown them—but being pirates, that seemed like a decent alternative to giving up their treasure. They all finally decided to let it go and survive. Then they swam as fast as they could.

Because the monsters were still after us. And they could swim as well.

I tried my best to swim away from them, but I couldn't do it with the trident.

"Let it go!" Belinda shouted to me.

"I can't!" I shouted back. "It's important!"

"It's just a dumb trident!" Belinda yelled back. "The merpeople can get another one!"

"That's not why it's important!" I yelled back. "I need it to glub glub glub glub."

That last part was the sound of me sinking into the water because I was too exhausted to swim anymore and the trident was too heavy to hold up.

As I sank beneath the surface, I could see what had once been the great city of Atlantis, now lying on the floor of the sea. Apparently, it had not been built quite as well as everyone had hoped.

I also saw the monsters closing in on me. There was a look of ravenous hunger in their eyes.

And then there was a look of fear.

The monsters suddenly all decided that they had other things to do and quickly swam away.

A great shadow fell over me.

I turned around . . .

And came face-to-face with the kraken.

CHAPTER SIXTEEN

The Kraken?!
Aaaaagh!!!!!

Actually, this wasn't as bad as it looks.

Remember, back in chapter 4, when Princess Piscina told us that the trident had magical powers, and that you could use it to make any sea creature do your bidding?

Well, the kraken was a sea creature.

The moment I had taken the trident from Calliope, I had felt its power. To be honest, it was kind of weird. I can't really explain it. I simply suddenly had the ability to communicate with the sea animals.

The first thing I did was make the kraken get to Atlantis as fast as it could and scare all the other monsters away.

The second thing I did was make the kraken agree not to eat us.

And since that was now taken care of, I called for some nice dolphins to come along and pick all the treasure up off the ocean floor.

Then I noticed that Rover was still tied to the tree where we had left him outside the city, only that area was now underwater, so I had a shark bite through the rope and free Rover before he drowned.

Then I had some seahorses lift me back to the surface. When I arrived there, Calliope and her pirates had taken control of their ship. (Since ships float, they were all that was left of Atlantis.) The pirates had their cannons aimed at us.

"Give us that treasure back or we'll blast you to smithereens!" Calliope ordered.

I considered having the kraken swallow them and their ship whole, but that seemed awfully nasty. So I decided to have an army of octopuses subdue the pirates instead.

It worked quite well.

Then I had the kraken let Belinda, Ferkle, Princess Grace, Rover, and me climb up onto its back.

From there, we had a good view of the previous location of Atlantis.

The Atlanteans had gathered on the distant shore. They had obviously escaped the arena before it collapsed and now seemed very upset about their city sinking below the sea. But since they had all been very eager to see us get eaten by ravenous beasts, I didn't feel that bad for them.

Prince Ruprecht and the royal family of Atlantis were clinging to some floating debris. Every member of the royal family was yelling at Prince Ruprecht at once.

"You destroyed our beautiful city!" the king shouted.

"You will never have our daughter's hand in marriage!" the queen yelled.

"You got me all wet!" Princess Petunia cried.

"You are a fool!" Prince Schmendrick hollered.

"It's not my fault!" Prince Ruprecht told them, then pointed toward us. "It's theirs! They ruin everything all the time! I hate them!" He glared at us and howled, "You haven't seen the last of me! I will get even with you if it's the last thing I ever do!"

Even though Ruprecht was in very bad shape at the moment, having sunk Atlantis and lost all of his stolen treasure, I knew to take his threats seriously. I had no doubt that he would cause my friends and me lots more trouble in the future.

But for now, we had things to do.

We had the octopuses take the pirates to shore, then commandeered their ship. Next, we fashioned a harness of seaweed to the kraken and hitched the ship to it as though it were an enormous, seagoing chariot. Then we had the kraken race us back to the Kingdom of Merland.

The kraken was so big and powerful, the trip didn't take long.

Word of what had happened to Atlantis had traveled quickly through the seas. By the time we reached the location of Merland, the entire kingdom was waiting at the surface for us, eager for the return of their precious trident.

We unhitched the pirate ship from the kraken, and before handing over the trident, I used its powers one last time to ask the enormous sea monster to leave us alone forever. The kraken nodded as though it understood and swam away.

After that, we returned the trident to King Neptuna. "You have served my people well, and we will always be indebted to you," he said. "In return for your help, I will guarantee you safe passage across the sea back to the Kingdom of Merryland."

"That's very kind of you," Belinda said. "But we aren't going back to Merryland right away."

Princess Grace, Ferkle, and I all looked at her, surprised. "We're not?" I asked.

"We can't." Belinda pointed to all the other treasures we had recovered from the pirates (who had stolen them from Prince Ruprecht, who had stolen them from the Kingdom of Dinkum, who had stolen them from their rightful owners.) "These treasures don't belong to us any more than they belonged to Ruprecht or the pirates. They need to be returned to their proper homes."

Princess Grace, Ferkle, and I all realized that she was right. Personally, I wasn't happy about this; I wanted to go home and have a few days without any peril or danger. But I had an even bigger problem at the moment: Princess Grace.

She had been staring at Belinda adoringly all throughout our voyage back to Merland. Now she put a hand to her heart and whispered to me, "Your cousin is the bravest, most honest, most thoughtful person I have ever met."

I realized that, by now, Princess Grace was completely smitten. ◁ IQ BOOSTER !

("Smitten" means "to be strongly attracted to someone." Princess Grace was staring at Belinda the same way that Prince Ruprecht looked at gold, or Sir Cumference looked at pie.)

She was obviously head over heels in love, and I knew that I couldn't let things keep going like this. Even though Belinda was going to be upset, I had to betray her trust.

"Princess Grace," I said. "There's something very

important that I need to tell you: Bull is a girl."

"I know," Princess Grace replied.

I gaped at her in astonishment. "You do?"

"Of course. In fact, I've known for a very long time."

THE QUEST OF DANGER

I thought back to all the conversations that I'd had with Princess Grace about Belinda. It now occurred to me that she had never referred to Belinda as a boy. She had never said "he" or "him" when referring to her. Although . . . "But you called her Bull," I said.

Princess Grace looked at me curiously. "Isn't that her name? I've never heard you call her anything else."

I realized that this was true as well. "Actually, her name is Belinda. . . ."

"Belinda," Princess Grace repeated happily, like it was a magical word.

I said, "So when you said you didn't want to marry any of those princes that we've met, that was really because . . ."

"All those princes were jerks," Princess Grace said. "I certainly don't want to marry a jerk. In fact, I'm not sure if I ever want to get married at all. But if I do, it's not going to be for wealth or power. I'm going to marry someone because I love them—and they love me."

I was very shocked by all of this—and yet pleased at the same time. I looked toward Belinda to see if she had overheard, but Belinda was distracted, talking to King Neptuna.

"Your decision to return these treasures to their rightful homes is a very brave and honorable one," the king was telling her. "You are obviously an excellent knight."

"She certainly is," Princess Grace said adoringly.

"I think so too," I agreed.

"Thanks," Belinda told King Neptuna, then looked over the pile of treasures on the deck of the ship. "There are so many things that need to be returned. Where should we start?"

King Neptuna said, "If you want to return the Cherished Ruby, Fazzini isn't that far away . . . but the trip will be treacherous."

Ferkle sighed heavily. "What else is new?"

I considered all the treasures. Returning them would be difficult . . . but it couldn't be *more* difficult than everything else we had been through, could it?

I then looked at my travel companions: Belinda, Ferkle, Princess Grace, and Rover. They had become my

closest friends. If anyone could handle the danger and trouble that lay ahead of us, it was them.

"Let's do it," I said.

The others cheered excitedly.

Even though we had successfully completed our quest, this wasn't quite . . .

THE END

Acknowledgments

I am extremely much beholden [TO BOOSTER!] to many, many people for their help with this book.

("Beholden" means owing thanks or having a duty to someone in return for a service they have provided. It also means "to dress like the main character from *Catcher in the Rye* for Halloween," which is a much funnier joke if you're an adult who has read that book.)

For starters, I'm beholden to my wonderful illustrator, Stacy Curtis, for bringing my characters and this world to life.

And I'm also beholden to my incredible team at Simon & Schuster: Krista Vitola, Justin Chanda, Lucy Ruth Cummins, Tom Daly, Erin Toller, Beth Parker, Roberta Stout, Kendra Levin, Alyza Liu, Anne Zafian, Lisa Moraleda, Jenica Nasworthy, Chava Wolin, Chrissy Noh, Ashley Mitchell, Brendon MacDonald, Nadia Almahdi, Christina Pecorale, Victor Iannone, Emily

Hutton, Emily Ritter, Theresa Pang, Michelle Leo, Nicole Benevento, and Amy Beaudoin.

Additional beholdenness goes to my amazing fellow writers (and support group): Sarah Mlynowski, James Ponti, Rose Brock, Julie Buxbaum, Julia DeVillers, Christina Soontornvat, Karina Yan Glaser, Max Brallier, and Gordon Korman.

Even more beholdenness goes to my agent, Jennifer Joel, and my assistant, Emma Chanen.

And finally, I could not be more thankful for my amazing children, Dashiell and Violet, who make me laugh and smile and burst with happiness every day. I love you both more than words can say.

About the Author and Illustrator

Stuart Gibbs is the *New York Times* bestselling author of the Charlie Thorne, FunJungle, Moon Base Alpha, Once Upon a Tim, and Spy School series. He has written screenplays, worked on a whole bunch of animated films, developed TV shows, been a newspaper columnist, and researched capybaras (the world's largest rodents). Stuart lives with his family in Los Angeles. You can learn more about what he's up to at StuartGibbs.com.

Stacy Curtis is a *New York Times* bestselling and award-winning illustrator, cartoonist, and printmaker. He has illustrated more than thirty-five children's books, including *Karate Kakapo*, which won the National Cartoonists Society's Book Illustration award. Stacy lives in the Chicago area with his wife, daughter, and two dogs.